Larry Gets Lost in Boston

Illustrated by John Skewes
Written by Michael Mullin and John Skewes

SASQUATCH BOOKS
SEATTLE

Manufactured in China by C&C Offset Printing Co. Ltd. Shenzhen,
Guangdong Province, in January 2013

Published by Sasquatch Books
17 16 15 14 13   9 8 7 6 5 4 3 2 1

Editor: Susan Roxborough
Project editor: Michelle Hope Anderson
Illustrations: John Skewes
Book design: Mint Design
Book composition: Sarah Plein

Library of Congress Cataloging-in-Publication Data is available.

ISBN-13: 978-1-57061-793-5

www.larrygetslost.com

SASQUATCH BOOKS
1904 Third Avenue, Suite 710
Seattle, WA 98101
(206) 467-4300
www.sasquatchbooks.com
custserv@sasquatchbooks.com

This is **Larry.**   This is **Pete.**

BOSTON HARBOR

They're bundled together
In the backseat.

They went into a tunnel
Then out the other side.
What adventure awaits
At the end of this ride?

Larry wondered,
What will we see in this place?
More important, he thought,
How does the food taste?

Out the window, Larry smelled salty sea air.
The breeze carried hints of seafood somewhere.

A bridge that seemed made of gigantic guitar strings
Was just one of the city's more spectacular things.

BOSTON

UNION OYSTER HOUSE

All done with the car,
They decided to park it.
With Larry on his leash,
They headed to Quincy Market.

Inside a big building
With a round copper top,
They found all kinds of restaurants
And places to shop.

While the family read menus
To find something to eat,
Larry's dog-tummy growled,
Then he spotted a treat!

Someone had dropped it
(But a dog doesn't care)
After eating what he'd found . . .

He realized
Pete wasn't there!

He had to get looking,
But where should he start?
Larry made mistakes,
But he was really quite smart.

In the ground he saw bricks
In a line, end to end.
Could this be a trail
That would lead to his friend?

THE FREEDOM TRAIL BOSTON

FANEUIL HALL
Built in 1742, this meeting hall was
the location of many great American
Revolution speeches. It is sometimes
called the Cradle of Liberty.

SAMUEL
ADAMS

THE OLD STATE HOUSE
On July 18, 1776, the Declaration of Independence was read from the second-floor balcony to a crowd below. It was also the site of the Boston Massacre on March 5, 1770.

BOSTON
COMMON

FOUNDED

1634

CITY OF BOSTON
DEPARTMENT OF PARKS AND RECREATION

Excited to find Pete,
Larry kept to his search.
He passed a redbrick building
And an old-fashioned church.

At the end of the line
Larry saw mostly green
As he entered a wide-open
Park kind of scene.

NORTH END

PAUL REVERE HOUSE
Revere was a prosperous silversmith and a patriot in the American Revolution who helped organize an alarm system to monitor the British military.

Meanwhile, Pete saw buildings
From a long-ago year,
Like a house once lived in
By a man named Revere.

What he really wanted to see
Was his dog's friendly face.
So they had to keep looking
In some other place.

They called Larry's name and
Listened for his bark . . .

OLD NORTH CHURCH
The steeple of this church is where the "One if by land, two if by sea" signal was said to be sent to Paul Revere in the famous poem "Paul Revere's Ride" by Henry Wadsworth Longfellow.

PAUL REVERE

PUBLIC GARDEN

Jack   Kack   Lack

. . . While Larry explored
That big grassy park.

He asked ducklings for help,
But they ignored his dog words.
So he crossed a lagoon
Filled with boats shaped like birds.

MAKE WAY FOR DUCKLINGS
Nine bronze duck statues pay tribute to the famous children's book by Robert McCloskey that takes place in Boston.

Mack

Nack

Ouack

Pack

Quack

SWAN BOATS
The famous pedal-powered Swan Boats have been taking people around the lake in the Public Garden since 1877.

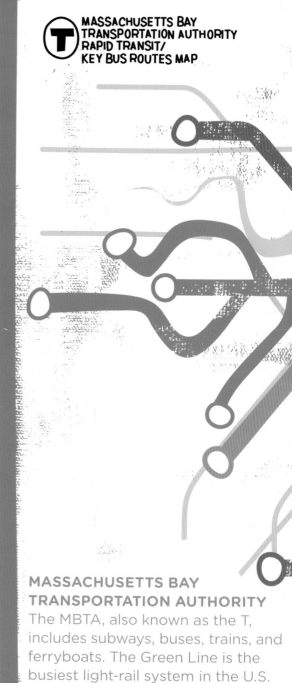

MASSACHUSETTS BAY TRANSPORTATION AUTHORITY
RAPID TRANSIT/
KEY BUS ROUTES MAP

**MASSACHUSETTS BAY
TRANSPORTATION AUTHORITY**
The MBTA, also known as the T,
includes subways, buses, trains, and
ferryboats. The Green Line is the
busiest light-rail system in the U.S.

Larry went down a staircase
And under the street
He saw all kinds of people,
Just not his friend Pete.

Red lines, orange lines,
What did they mean?
Larry hopped on a train
That was painted bright green.

A baseball stadium seemed huge
To lost little Larry.
He faced a Green Monster
(But it wasn't so scary).

He then ran by a river
And heard musical notes,
While people rowed quickly
In long, skinny boats.

HATCH MEMORIAL SHELL
Originally built as a temporary concert venue in 1928, the permanent shell was built in 1940 and is home to the annual 4th of July concert by the Boston Pops Orchestra.

FENWAY PARK
Home to the Boston Red Sox since 1912, it is the oldest operating ballpark in the U.S. The 37-foot-high left-field wall is called the Green Monster.

JOHN HANCOCK TOWER

LISTEN MY CHILDREN AND YOU SHALL HEAR OF THE M
OF APRIL, IN SEVENTY-FIVE; HARDLY A MAN IS NOW

On a bridge that looked like
Salt-and-pepper shakers,
Larry barked for assistance
But there weren't any takers.

From the bridge he saw buildings,
Some old and some new.
The biggest one reflected
The others in blue.

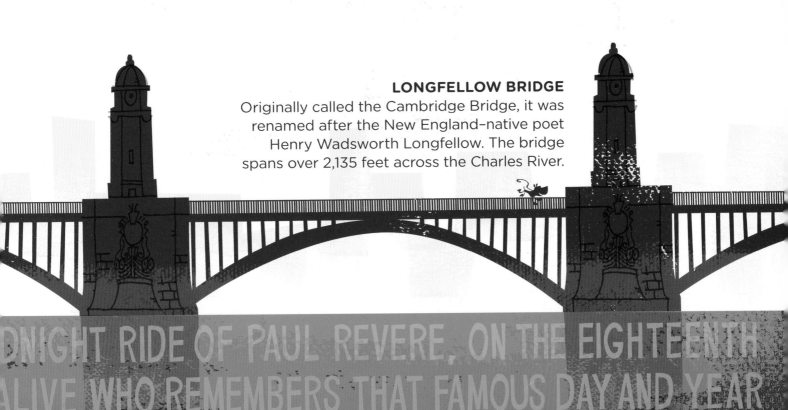

LONGFELLOW BRIDGE
Originally called the Cambridge Bridge, it was
renamed after the New England–native poet
Henry Wadsworth Longfellow. The bridge
spans over 2,135 feet across the Charles River.

DNIGHT RIDE OF PAUL REVERE, ON THE EIGHTEENTH
ALIVE WHO REMEMBERS THAT FAMOUS DAY AND YEAR

At his next stop, a big
Dinosaur was standing guard.
But getting past him
Wasn't all that hard.

On another bridge
Not too far away,
Pete wished Larry could see
All his discoveries that day.

MUSEUM OF SCIENCE
Opened at its current location in 1951, this is
one of the oldest science museums in the U.S.
It has hundreds of interactive exhibits.

CHARLESTOWN BRIDGE
The first official ferry crossing of the
Charles River was at this site in 1630.
The current bridge was built in 1900.

Inside the museum
Larry saw lightning!
It was bright and loud
(And a little frightening).

Just when Larry's hopes
Were starting to fade,
A college student
Came to his aid.

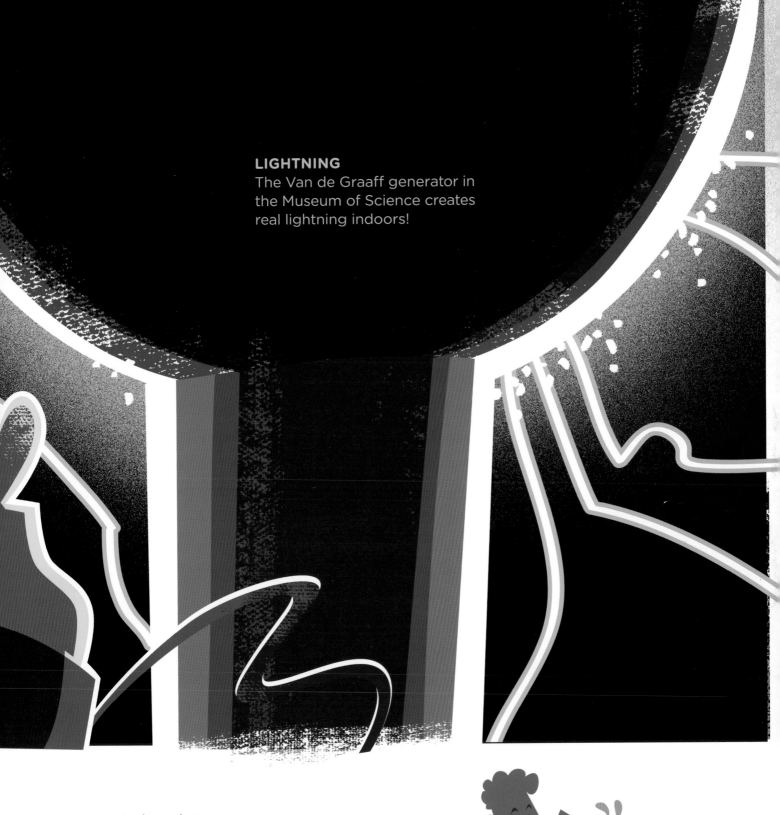

LIGHTNING
The Van de Graaff generator in
the Museum of Science creates
real lightning indoors!

He picked Larry up
And checked his dog collar.
What luck! thought Larry
As he licked the young scholar.

They didn't see Larry
On an old sailing ship.
Pete wished his pal could share
In the fun of this trip.

While Pete was feeling sad,
He heard a beeping sound.
It was Dad's phone!
Larry had been found!

USS CONSTITUTION
Built for the US Navy in 1794, this wooden ship
earned the nickname Old Ironsides, because
instead of making holes, enemy cannonballs just
bounced off the ship's sides.

BUNKER HILL MONUMENT

This 221-foot monument was built to commemorate the Battle of Bunker Hill in the Revolutionary War. Visitors can climb the 294 steps inside and look out a window at the top. A railway was built in 1826 just to bring the granite from Quincy.

They arranged to meet
At a famous place.
Pete could hardly wait
To see Larry's face.

They drove up a hill
To the end of the street,
Where Larry jumped up
And landed on Pete!

They slept as the car
Drove slowly away.
It had been a very
Adventurous day!

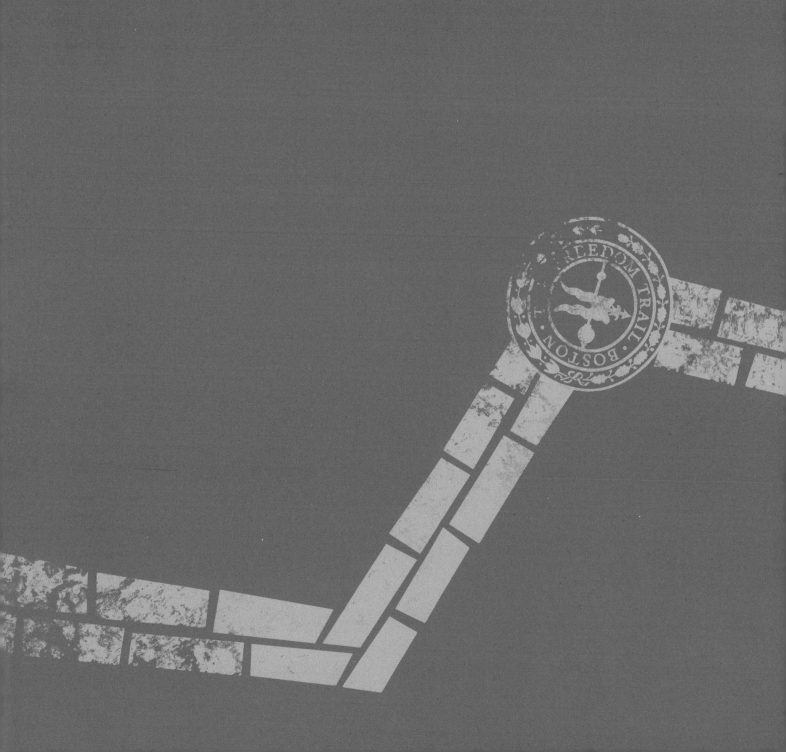

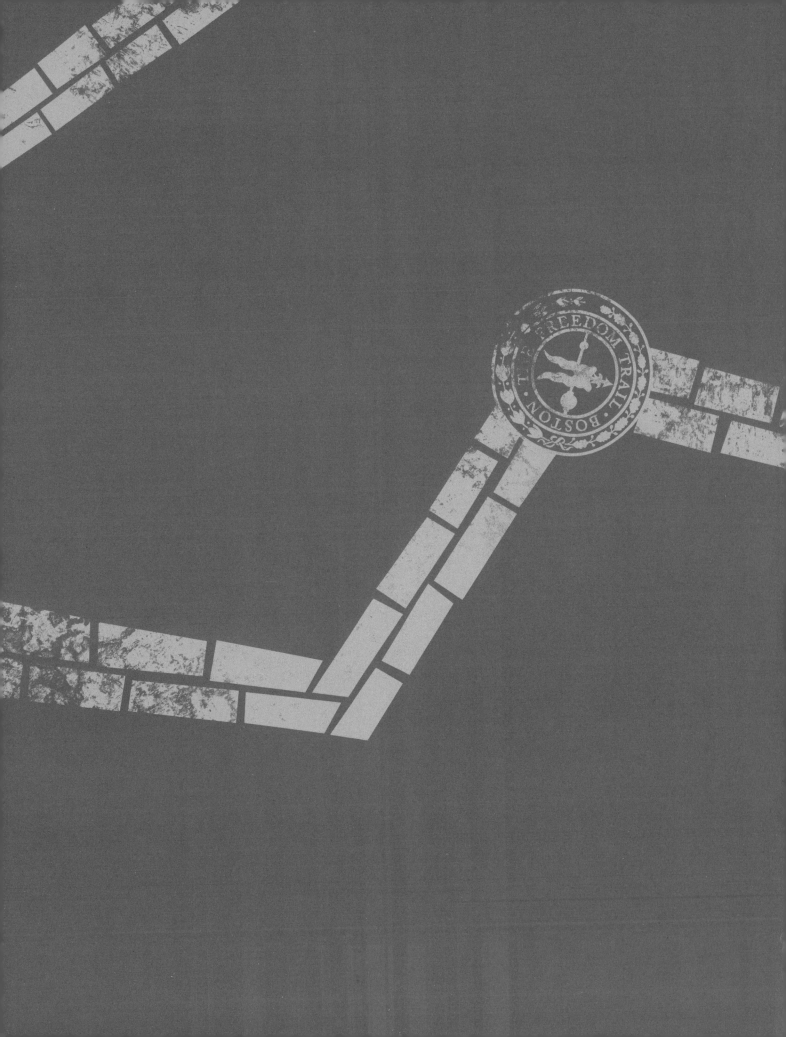